This Little Tiger book
belongs to:

This

You m

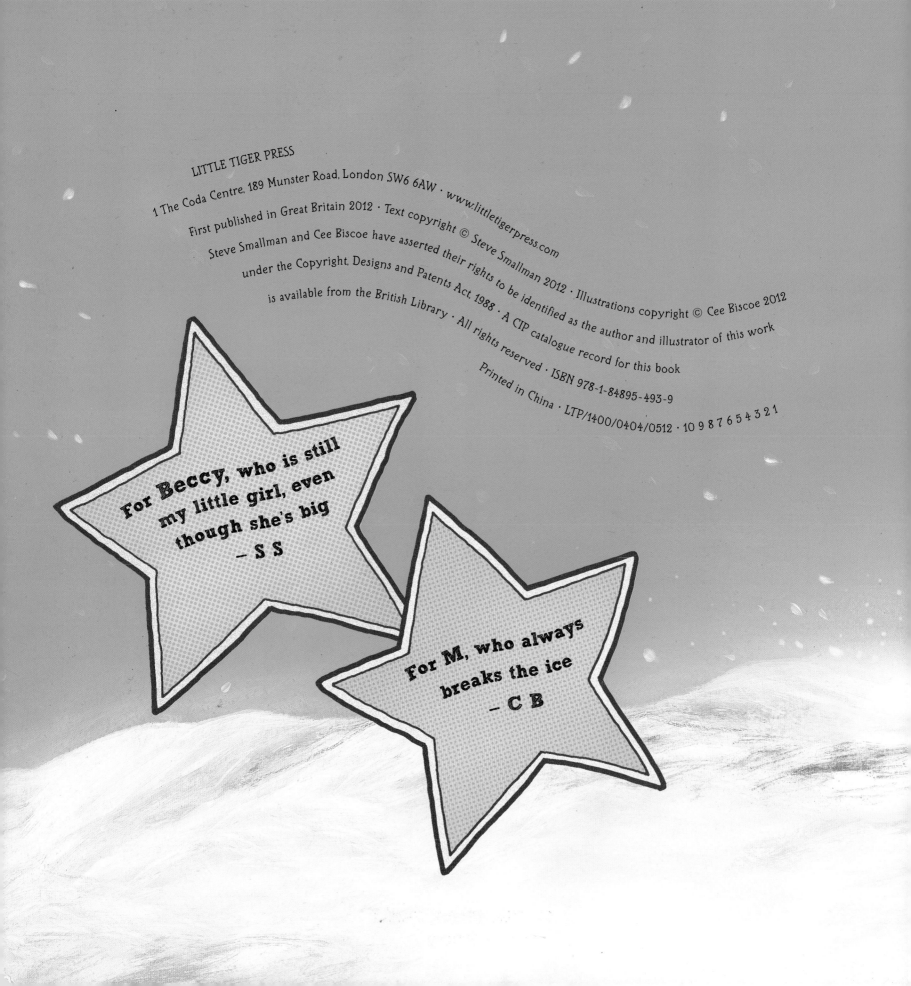

LITTLE TIGER PRESS
1 The Coda Centre, 189 Munster Road, London SW6 6AW · www.littletigerpress.com

First published in Great Britain 2012 · Text copyright © Steve Smallman 2012 · Illustrations copyright © Cee Biscoe 2012

Steve Smallman and Cee Biscoe have asserted their rights to be identified as the author and illustrator of this work

under the Copyright, Designs and Patents Act, 1988 · A CIP catalogue record for this book

is available from the British Library · All rights reserved · ISBN 978-1-84895-493-9

Printed in China · LTP/1400/0404/0512 · 10 9 8 7 6 5 4 3 2 1

For Beccy, who is still
my little girl, even
though she's big
– S S

For M, who always
breaks the ice
– C B

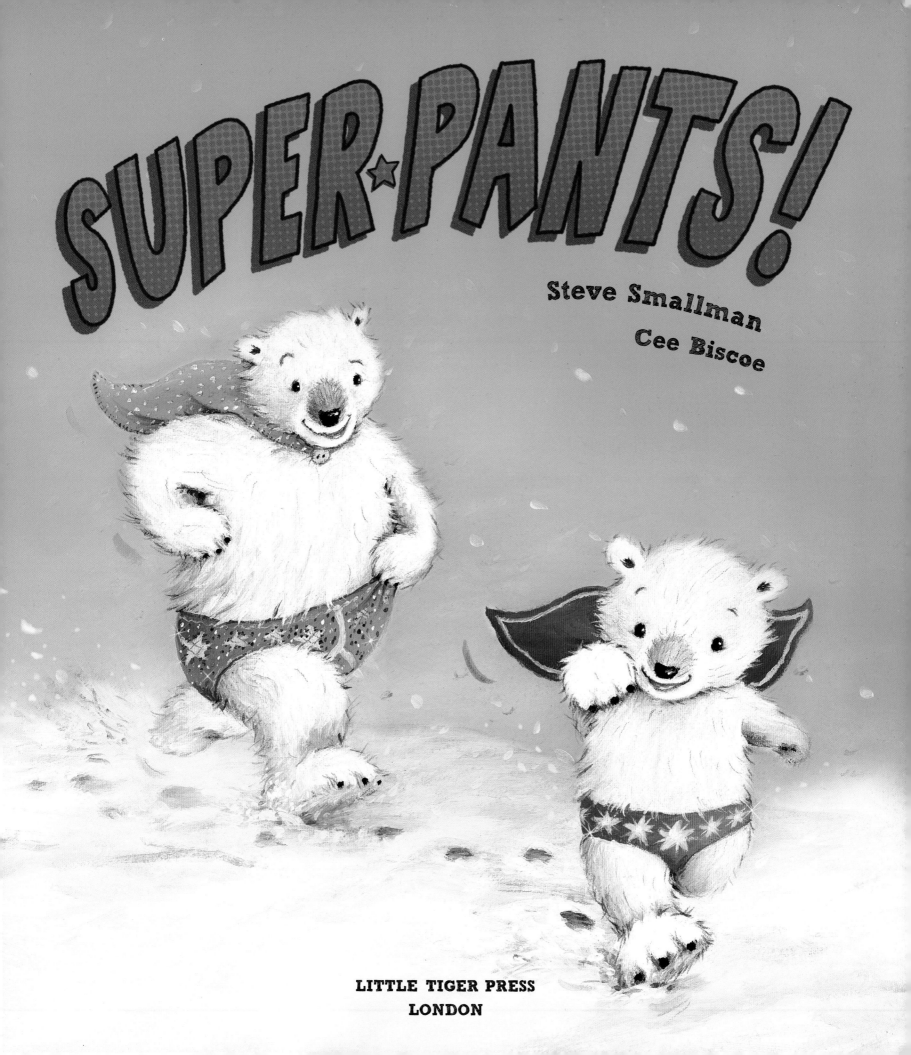

SUPER★PANTS!

Steve Smallman

Cee Biscoe

LITTLE TIGER PRESS

LONDON

It was Christmas day. Mummy, Daddy and little Lola polar bear were opening their presents.

Mummy had a lovely scarf.

Lola had SUPERHERO PANTS!

"Look!" she cried. "I'm Super Lola polar bear!"

"You look fantastic!" smiled Daddy. "Now, what could MY present be?"

"Superhero pants?!

I didn't think these came
in my size?" said Daddy.

"They **don't**," replied Mummy.
"I made them just for YOU! There's a cape too."

"Now we're **both** superheroes
in our super pants!" cried Lola.
"Let's go and rescue something!"

"Off you go, Super Daddy!" chuckled Mummy.
"See you later."

Super Lola polar bear raced off,
looking for adventure!

Super Daddy lumbered after her
with his cape flapping in the breeze.

"I'm on top of the world!"

she shouted.

"Be careful, Lola," said Daddy.

But Lola wasn't listening.
She was too busy being
the **best** superhero **ever.**

"And I'm super **loud** toooo!"

she yelled.

"You certainly **are!**" said Daddy.
But Lola was off again . . .

"Daddy, that birdie's stuck!" gasped Lola. "Let's **rescue** him!"

"Squawk!"

She scrambled up to reach,

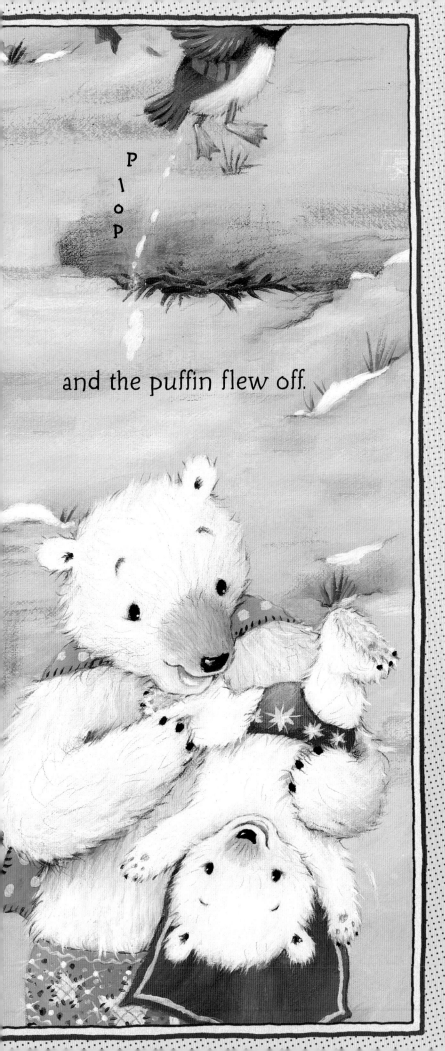

P
l
o
p

and the puffin flew off.

"Hooray! We **did it**, Daddy!" cheered Lola. "Let's go and help someone else!"

After a very busy morning, Daddy sat down
for a rest. It was hard work being a superhero!

"Daddy, look!" cried Lola.
"Those penguins are floating out to sea!
Let's rescue them!"

"Erm, I don't think . . ." replied Daddy,
but it was too late.

"Lola!" shouted Daddy.
"Slow down!"

As Lola tripped, Super Daddy
did a **super leap** and
caught her just in time.

"Super Lola to the

They shot off the cliff with a WHOOSH, and flew straight towards the penguins.

"rescue!" she yelled.

ASH!

Daddy and Lola landed on the ice and eight grumpy penguins sploshed into the water!
"Oops! Sorry!" said Daddy.

"Don't worry, penguins," cried Lola.
"We've come to **save** you! My daddy will
carry you on his back. Won't you, Daddy?"
"Yes," sighed Daddy. "Why not?"

Back on shore, Daddy dried the penguins
with his superhero cape.
"Are you all right?" he asked.
The penguins weren't sure.

"Would a little Christmas dinner make you
feel better?" asked Daddy.
The penguins were sure that it would.

By now it was getting dark,
and little Lola was feeling a bit tired, so Daddy
wrapped her up and gave her a big cuddle.
"Let's go home," he said.

Mummy said it was a lovely surprise to have so many new friends for Christmas dinner. "Have you had a super time?" she asked. "Oh yes, Mummy, it's been my best Christmas ever!" said Lola. "Me and my Daddy are the **greatest superheroes** in the **whole wide world!**"

More SUPER books from Little Tiger Press!

Before We Go To Bed
Sue Mongredien · Cee Biscoe

The Not-So Scary Snorklum
Paul Bright · Jane Chapman

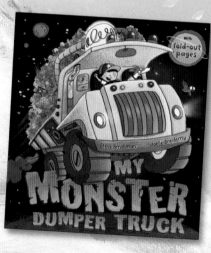

with fold-out pages

MY MONSTER DUMPER TRUCK
Steve Smallman · Joëlle Dreidemy

Who's Afraid of the Big Bad Bunny?
Steve Smallman · Caroline Pedler

PAUL BRIGHT
CHARLIE'S SUPERHERO UNDERPANTS
Lee Wildish

Too Hot to Hug!
Steve Smallman · Cee Biscoe

For information regarding any of the above titles or for our catalogue, please contact us:
Little Tiger Press, 1 The Coda Centre,
189 Munster Road, London SW6 6AW
Tel: 020 7385 6333 · Fax: 020 7385 7333
E-mail: info@littletiger.co.uk
www.littletigerpress.com